# PUTTING THE WORLD TO SLEEP

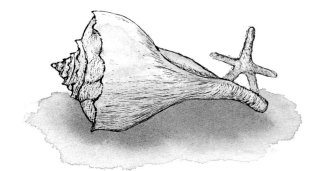

# PUTTING THE WORLD TO SLEEP

*Shelley Moore Thomas* ❧ *Pictures by Bonnie Christensen*

Houghton Mifflin Company

Boston 1995

Text copyright © 1995 by Shelley Moore Thomas
Illustrations copyright © 1995 by Bonnie Christensen

*Library of Congress Cataloging-in-Publication Data*

Thomas, Shelley Moore.
  Putting the world to sleep / by Shelley Moore Thomas ; illustrated
by Bonnie Christensen.
      p.   cm.
  Summary: As the moon comes up, the crickets sing, the stars shine,
a fireplace glows, a mother sings, and a baby yawns.
  ISBN 0-395-71283-1
  [1. Night—Fiction.   2. Bedtime—Fiction.]   I. Christensen,
Bonnie, ill.   II. Title.
PZ7.T369458Pu   1995         94-28675
[E]—dc20                     CIP
                             AC

Printed in the United States of America

BVG   10  9  8  7  6  5  4  3  2  1

The moon climbs over the mountain each night,
putting the world to sleep.

The crickets start singing farewell to the day,
as the moon climbs over the mountain each night,
putting the world to sleep.

The stars shine across the sea and the land,
as the crickets start singing farewell to the day,
as the moon climbs over the mountain each night,
putting the world to sleep.

Darkness falls over the trees and the roofs,
as the stars shine across the sea and the land,
as the crickets start singing farewell to the day,
as the moon climbs over the mountain each night,
putting the world to sleep.

The fireplace glows in an old brown house,
as darkness falls over the trees and the roofs,
as the stars shine across the sea and the land,
as the crickets start singing farewell to the day,
as the moon climbs over the mountain each night,
putting the world to sleep.

A big dog lounges on a tattered red rug,
as the fireplace glows in an old brown house,
as darkness falls over the trees and the roofs,
as the stars shine across the sea and the land,
as the crickets start singing farewell to the day,
as the moon climbs over the mountain each night,
putting the world to sleep.

A mommy is humming a lullaby,
as a big dog lounges on a tattered red rug,
as the fireplace glows in an old brown house,
as darkness falls over the trees and the roofs,
as the stars shine across the sea and the land,
as the crickets start singing farewell to the day,
as the moon climbs over the mountain each night,
putting the world to sleep.

A dreamy-eyed baby yawns big and wide,
as a mommy is humming a lullaby,
as a big dog lounges on a tattered red rug,
as the fireplace glows in an old brown house,
as darkness falls over the trees and the roofs,
as the stars shine across the sea and the land,
as the crickets start singing farewell to the day,
as the moon climbs over the mountain each night,
putting the world to sleep.

"Good night, world."

"Good night."